yoko geri kekomi
side thrust kick

nukite
spear hand thrust

yoi
ready

kokutsu dachi
back stance

zenkutsu dachi
front stance

soto uke
outside block

gedan barai
downward block

shuto uke
knife hand block

yoko tobi geri
jump kick

I'm Maya, and
I want to be a karate kid!

To John,
for the love,
support,
and inspiration
he gives every day

• First U.S. edition 2020 • Library of Congress Catalog Card Number pending ISBN 978-1-5362-1457-4 • This book was typeset in Intro Regular Alt. The illustrations were done in pencil and colored digitally. • Candlewick Press, 99 Dover Street, Somerville, Massachusetts 02144 • www.candlewick.com • Printed in Dongguan, Guangdong, China • 19 20 21 22 23 24 TLF 10 9 8 7 6 5 4 3 2 1

KARATE KIDS

HOLLY STERLING

CANDLEWICK PRESS

Today I wake up bright and early.
It's Saturday, which means
I have my karate class!

I wear my crisp white uniform, which is called a **gi**.

I find my white belt (for beginners like me).

And I'm ready. Let's go!

Dad takes me to the **dojo**.
That's where we practice our karate moves.

All my karate friends are
on their way, too.

First, we take our shoes
and socks off.

One

and two!

Then we bow to our **sensei**.
She's our teacher.

Sensei asks us to warm up our bodies
from the tops of our heads
to the tips of our toes.

Finja bends down.
Patrick jumps up.

Hana swings her arms from side to side.

I can't touch my toes yet, but I stretch as far as I can go.

Then we practice our blocks.

Age uke
blocks the head.

Soto uke
blocks the stomach.

And **gedan barai**
blocks down low.

I get a little mixed up with my arms,
but Sensei is there to give me
some extra help.

I'm excited to show off
my balance.

But I start to wibble and
wobble . . .

and
bump!

When Sensei says **"Yoi,"**
I know it's time to show her
what I've got.

HAI-YAH!

I **kiai** at the top of my voice.

Look, I'm a karate kid!

To wind down again,
we kneel and close our eyes.
We call this **mokuso** time.

We breathe in . . .
and out . . .
calmly and slowly.

In . . . out.   In . . . out.

Whoa! Everyone is here to pick us up already. Karate class always goes so quickly.

As I leave the dojo,
I see Tomoko, one of the big kids,
practicing her kata.
She is smooth and graceful.
She has a black belt!

Oh, I really want to be as good
as she is when I grow up.

And maybe I will be.

Hello!

I began karate when I was ten years old. Soon I was taking part in karate competitions all over the world, winning medals at both the European and world levels. In 2013, I became the first female athlete to be crowned Grand Champion two years in a row at the Karate Union of Great Britain's National Championships.

I have now retired from competitive karate, but I teach at my own dojos, and the children whom I have taught over the years have inspired the characters in this story. There is nothing that I love more than teaching. Karate not only helps to improve fitness and flexibility, but it also teaches confidence, mindfulness, compassion and respect. It's also a great way to make friends!

To all those karate kids out there, keep challenging yourself! And to those about to go to their first karate class, I look forward to welcoming you to the karate family!

J Sterling

kiba dachi
horse riding stance

ushiro geri
back kick

musubi dachi
informal stance

seiza
kneel

yoko empi uchi
side elbow strike

age empi uchi
rising elbow strike

mae geri
front kick

age uke
rising block

oi zuki
stepping lunge